Dear Parents and Educators,

Welcome to Penguin Young Readers! As pc •
know that each child develops at his or her own
speech, critical thinking, and, of **JER Meiste**
Readers recognizes this fact. As **Meister, Cari**
book is assigned a traditional ea **Hi-ho, Tiny**
Guided Reading Level (A–P). Bc
the right book for your child. Ple
for specific leveling information.
esteemed authors and illustrato
fascinating nonfiction, and more.

Hi-Ho, Tiny

This book is perfect for an **Emergent Reader** who:
• can read in a left-to-right and top-to-bottom progression;
• can recognize some beginning and ending letter sounds;
• can use picture clues to help tell the story; and
• can understand the basic plot and sequence of simple stories.

Here are some **activities** you can do during and after reading this book:
• Picture Clues: Sometimes pictures can tell you something about the story that is not told in words. Look at the pictures on pages 22–23, 24–25, and 26–27. Each picture gives you more information about why Tiny and Elliot are dressed in costume. Can you tell where Tiny and Elliot are going? Turn to page 28 to find out!
• Make Connections: In this story, Tiny and Elliot get dressed up in costumes. Have you ever worn a costume? Write a paragraph about a time you wore a costume.

Remember, sharing the love of reading with a child is the best gift you can give!

—Bonnie Bader, EdM
  Penguin Young Readers program

*Penguin Young Readers are leveled by independent reviewers applying the standards developed by Irene Fountas and Gay Su Pinnell in *Matching Books to Readers: Using Leveled Books in Guided Reading*, Heinemann, 1999.

For Catherine—CM

PENGUIN YOUNG READERS
Published by the Penguin Group
Penguin Group (USA) LLC, 375 Hudson Street, New York, New York 10014, USA

USA | Canada | UK | Ireland | Australia | New Zealand | India | South Africa | China

penguin.com
A Penguin Random House Company

Text copyright © 2015 by Cari Meister. Illustrations copyright © 2015 by Richard D. Davis. All rights
reserved. Published by Penguin Young Readers, an imprint of Penguin Group (USA) LLC,
345 Hudson Street, New York, New York 10014. Manufactured in China.

Library of Congress Cataloging-in-Publication Data is available.

ISBN 978-0-448-48291-0 (pbk)   10 9 8 7 6 5 4 3 2 1
ISBN 978-0-448-48292-7 (hc)   10 9 8 7 6 5 4 3 2 1

PENGUIN YOUNG READERS

LEVEL

EMERGENT
READER

1

Hi-Ho, TiNY

by Cari Meister
illustrated by Rich Davis

Penguin Young Readers
An Imprint of Penguin Group (USA) LLC

Get up, Tiny!

It is a big day.

I have my vest.

I have my hat.

I have my boots.

What will you wear?

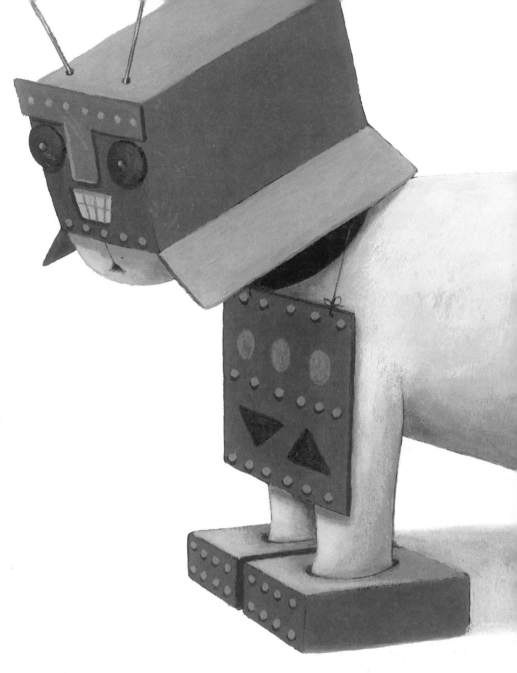

No, you cannot see.

No, you cannot walk.

I know!

You can be my horse.

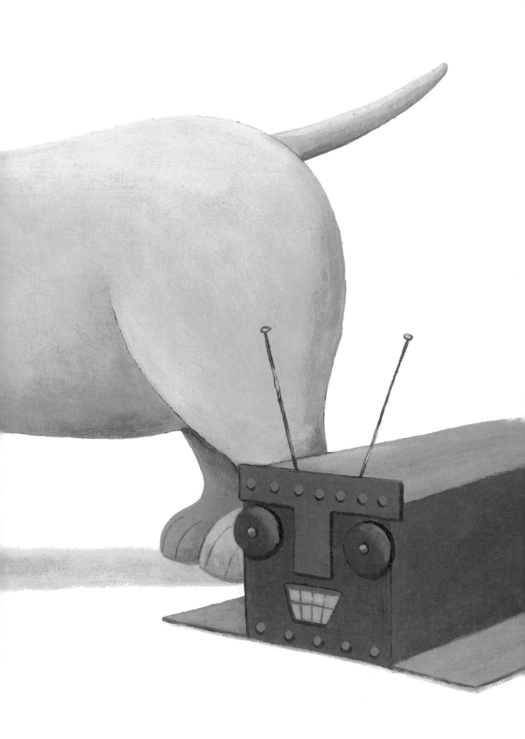

Stay, Tiny.

Oh no!

Now I am up.

Hi-ho, Tiny!

Away!

18

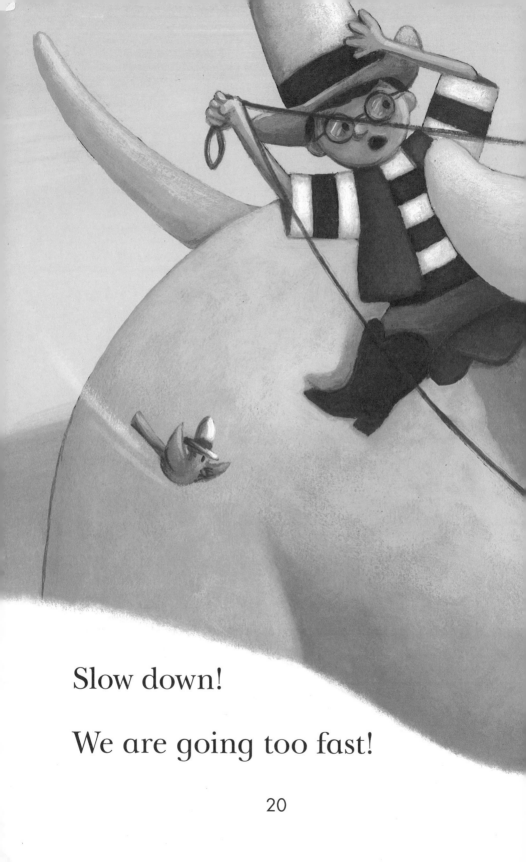

Slow down!

We are going too fast!

Oh no!

Watch out for the tree!

Watch out for the balloons!

Watch out for the float!

See, Tiny?

Today is the parade!

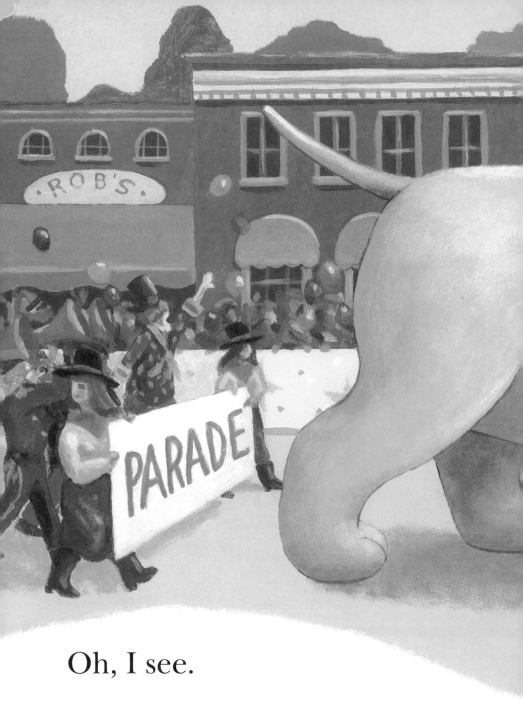

Oh, I see.

You want to be first.

Hi-ho, Tiny!

Away!